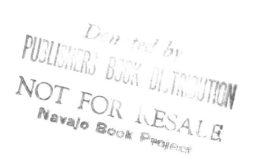

THINGS WON'T BE THE SAME

BY THE SAME AUTHOR

A Private Matter

Kathryn Ewing

Things Won't Be the Same

Harcourt Brace Jovanovich, Publishers
San Diego   New York   London

Requests for permission to make copies of
any part of the work should be mailed to:
Permissions, Harcourt Brace Jovanovich, Inc.,
757 Third Avenue, New York, New York 10017.

Printed in the United States of America

LIBRARY OF CONGRESS CATALOGING IN PUBLICATION DATA
Ewing, Kathryn.
Things won't be the same.
SUMMARY: Upset by her mother's coming remarriage,
10-year-old Marcy is upset further when she learns she'll
be staying with her father whom she's never known.
        [1.   Remarriage—Fiction]   I.   Title.
PZ7.E96Th   [Fic]   80-7982
                ISBN 0-15-285663-3

                        B   C   D   E

1

The house in Linden was very different from the one back in Glenview. Right away Marcy could see this. She had hoped that when her mother and Mr. William Compton got married, they would fix up the 9 Morris Avenue house where Marcy and her mother had been living for as long as Marcy could remember. Then she could stay in her own school, and except for Mr. Compton's being around a lot, things wouldn't change much at all.

But as soon as Mr. Compton turned into Dell Lane, slowed down the car, and drove up to the curb, Marcy's heart sank. No matter what her mother and Mr. Compton did to the Morris Avenue house, it would never look like this one. There was simply no comparison, no comparison at all. If Marcy had any doubts, they vanished when her mother turned to Mr. Compton and said, "Bill, that's not the color we want on the front door."

Right that minute Marcy knew she could

say good-bye to Morris Avenue and Glenview and Kingswood Elementary School even without Mr. Compton's turning around and saying, "Well, Marcy, how do you like your new home?"

Fortunately her mother laughed and said, "Oh, Bill! She hasn't seen it yet!"

Marcy was glad she didn't have to answer because she could tell Mr. Compton liked it a lot, and she didn't want to hurt his feelings. But down deep in her heart she didn't like it at all.

Not that there was anything wrong with the looks of it. Walking through the rooms behind her mother and Mr. Compton, she could see that it was perfect. A brand-new perfect house still smelling of paint and plaster, with her own room even painted her favorite sky blue, and if only it could have been on a street back in Glenview, everything would have been perfect. But it wasn't. It was in Linden, ten miles away.

After they walked through the house, they stepped out the back door and stood on the cement patio. There was nothing but mud all around, but Mr. Compton and her mother pointed to rosebushes and tulips, just as though they were already growing up out of the ground.

"I want a perennial bed, too, Bill," said

her mother. "After we're married, I'll have more time."

Marcy's mother was always saying "after we're married . . ." even though they wouldn't be married until next September, which was almost four months away. Marcy tried not to think about it. She tried to forget about her mother's getting married, about moving away from Glenview and going to a new school. But it was hard to keep her mind off it with her mother's talking about it all the time.

When they got through looking at the house, Mr. Compton said, "Now, Marcy, we'll take a look at your school." He said it as though it were her school already, as though she were already going there.

"It's not my school yet," she reminded him sharply.

"But it will be, Marcy," said her mother. "And please don't talk fresh."

Marcy had been hanging over the front seat of the car with her chin propped on her hands, but now she sat back and stared out the window. She didn't want to see the school. She didn't care one bit what it looked like or anything about it. It would never take the place of Kingswood Elementary.

And Linden would never take the place of Glenview. Already she could see that.

For one thing, Linden wasn't a real town at all. It was just hundreds and jillions of houses with a big shopping center in the middle and a huge highway with cars and trucks speeding by. She'd never be able to hop on her bike to go to the movies or the library or whatever she had in mind—the way she did in Glenview. It just wasn't like Glenview at all.

However, when they turned off the highway into the curving drive of the John Wellington Elementary School, she had to admit the school was nice. It was faced with pink brick and was long and low with lots of windows, but the surprising thing about it was that it was almost identical to Kingswood Elementary, and when she first saw it, her heart gave a leap.

"It looks like Kingswood!" she cried.

"Yes, it does," said Mr. Compton. "You're going to feel right at home."

Marcy didn't answer. She liked Mr. Compton okay and knew he was trying to make things better, but somehow its being a place that looked almost like Kingswood Elementary only made everything worse.

That night after she'd taken her bath and gotten into bed, her mother came up the stairs and sat on the side of her bed.

"Linden isn't far away, you know, Marcy," she said, just as though she had been reading Marcy's thoughts all day.

"Ten miles," said Marcy. "Coming back I saw the sign. Glenview, ten miles."

"Ten miles isn't far."

"It might as well be a jillion!" Suddenly just thinking about it brought tears to Marcy's eyes. "Nothing's going to be the same."

"I only meant you can visit back and forth."

"But that's not the same!"

Her mother waited a minute. Then she nodded her head as though she had made up her mind about something. "No, Marcy," she said. "Things won't be the same."

Usually it pleased Marcy when her mother agreed with her, but this time it made her stomach feel queer. Marcy sucked in her breath real sharply. Even her mother had to admit things wouldn't be the same.

2

The next day, however, standing beside
Wendy on the playground of the Kingswood
Elementary School, Marcy surprised herself
by the way she talked. She always told everything to Wendy because Wendy was her best
friend, but today she was really surprised to
hear herself say, "I've got a neat bedroom.
Sky blue."

"Ummm!" replied Wendy, as though
Marcy's bedroom were something good to eat.

"And there's a fireplace in the den." She
went on to tell about the whole house, includ-
ing the rosebushes and tulips that weren't
even planted yet in the backyard.

"Ummm!" said Wendy. "Luck-eee!"

Going back into Miss MacMannes's Grade
4B classroom, Marcy started to think about
Wendy's calling her lucky. Was she? She
began to concentrate on the good things such
as having a shiny new yellow and white
bathroom all to herself. And if nothing else

had happened, she might have gone right on feeling lucky, right through the wedding and moving to Linden and going to a new school.

But then everything changed. Right out of the blue everything changed in the worst possible way.

It was after supper, and they were still sitting at the kitchen counter—the way they always did while her mother finished her coffee and Marcy finished her milk.

"Marcy, I have something to tell you," her mother said. "Bill and I are going to be married in June."

"June!" Marcy spluttered because somehow she had inhaled instead of swallowing, and a fine froth of milk had traveled up her nose.

Her mother didn't even notice. Her face was bright pink. "That's right, Marcy. June 10. Three weeks away."

"But you said September!"

"I know. But we can move up the date. Bill's divorce has come through."

Marcy was trying to get used to this idea when her mother said, "There's something else, too. It's about your father."

For a minute Marcy thought her mother meant Mr. Compton because, of course, once he and her mother got married, he would be her stepfather. But then she remembered her real father out in California, and all at once the palms of her hands got sweaty. "My father!"

"Yes, Marcy. He would like you to visit him while Bill and I are on our honeymoon."

Marcy's mouth dropped open. "In California?"

"Yes."

Little prickles broke out on Marcy's skin. She didn't know her father very well. Since he lived so far away, she had seen him only once—when he and his new wife had come to Glenview last year and had taken Marcy to Philadelphia for the weekend.

"For a month. Bill and I will be away for a month."

Marcy knew all about the honeymoon. Everything had been decided. Mr. Compton and her mother were going to Mexico, and Marcy was supposed to stay with Wendy. But now everything was being changed. Tears stung her eyes. "You promised I could stay with Wendy."

"I know I promised, Marcy. And you may still do that if you prefer. But it might be fun to visit your father for a while. He very much wants to see you, and I'm sure he'll plan all sorts of nice things for you to do. But you decide. He'll be calling tomorrow night, and it's up to you."

More and more these days her mother was

saying, "It's up to you." Marcy wished she would stop it. She didn't like everything being up to her, except that she was certainly glad it was up to her about visiting her father in California because she wasn't going to go.

"Will you tell him I don't want to?" she asked.

"Honey," said her mother, "he'll want to talk to you."

"But what will I tell him?"

"Simply say, 'Thank you, but I'm going to be spending the month with my friend Wendy.' "

"But suppose he gets mad!"

"I'm sure he won't, Marcy. I'm sure he'll be disappointed, but I doubt very much he'll get mad."

"But suppose he does!"

"Gracious, Marcy. Then he does!"

Marcy could see that her mother was getting mad, so she went into the living room to watch TV. All the next day, she went over and over the sentence in her mind. *Thank you, but I'm going to be spending the month with my friend Wendy.*

She must have said it a million times. Once when she tried to think of it, she couldn't remember it at all. Another time it came out: *Thank you, but I'm going to be spending the month with my wend Fendy.*

If she said it that way to her father, she'd

9

just die! But when the telephone rang and her father said, "How about coming on out to California?" she didn't mention Wendy at all. The only thing she said was "okay."

"I'm going to California after all," she told her mother after she hung up the phone and went out to the kitchen.

Her mother wasn't nearly as surprised as Marcy was. Her mother didn't appear to be surprised at all. "That's nice," she said and went right on cleaning out the refrigerator, just as though nothing whatever had happened.

It was Marcy's turn to be mad. "Nice!" she cried. "You're going to let me go all the way out to California all alone?"

"Well, Marcy," said her mother, "you won't exactly be traveling by horse and wagon. Aunt Peg will put you on the plane at this end, and the flight attendant will hand you right over to your father in San Francisco."

"Nobody has to hand me over to my father. I'm not a baby."

"Then please stop acting like one," said her mother. "And don't talk fresh."

That night in bed Marcy heard her mother and Mr. Compton down in the living room discussing her trip to California.

"She doesn't really want to go," her

mother was saying. "She's a little nervous about being with her father, I'm afraid."

"Don't worry about it," said Mr. Compton. "She'll get over it."

"I know she'll get over it," said her mother sharply. "But I can't help worrying a little, Bill."

It was the first time Marcy had ever heard her mother speak sharply to Mr. Compton. She wouldn't have believed Mr. Compton could ever make her mother mad.

3

The next day in the schoolyard she told Wendy about going to California.

"Luck-eee!" Wendy said.

In a way Marcy had to agree—especially about flying out there all alone. She had to admit it was kind of neat.

"So we're going to lose our visitor!" said Wendy's mother later that day.

"Aunt Peg," as Marcy called her, had picked up the two girls in the car after school because Marcy's mother had gone into Philadelphia to buy her wedding dress and wouldn't be home for supper.

"Yes," Marcy said.

"Out to visit your daddy and his new wife. Won't that be nice?"

Marcy didn't say anything. She just kept drinking the Hawaiian Punch Aunt Peg had fixed for them because she didn't know whether it would be nice or not.

———

That night around nine o'clock her mother picked her up at Aunt Peg's and brought her home. In the back seat of the car was a big dress box, with a hat box beside it.

When they got inside the house, her mother said, "Want to see my wedding dress?"

It was really pretty—pale blue with a wide skirt. In the hat box was a big blue straw hat. Her mother held the dress up to her and put on the hat.

"It's really pretty, Mom," Marcy told her. "I like it a lot."

"Well, thank goodness that's that!" said her mother.

Marcy knew that now her mother would be able to cross *wedding gown* off the list she kept on her bureau. There weren't many more things to be crossed off. Time was really running out.

"So how come you got divorced from my father?" Marcy asked suddenly.

Her mother's hands went still. Then she sat right down on the sofa in the middle of the tissue paper and all.

"You have a perfect right to ask," she said, as though she had been waiting for this question for a long time. "Your father and I were very young when we got married. Too young. We were only eighteen. We didn't get along together. It wasn't anyone's fault—not your father's nor mine. We just didn't get along."

"Are you sorry now?"

"I was sorry then, but I'm not sorry now. Now I want to be married to Bill. Just as your father wants to be married to Ginny."

As usual, her mother must have told Mr. Compton about this conversation. One thing that really got to Marcy these days was the way her mother had to tell Mr. Compton every little thing. "Marcia, about your parents' divorce," he said the next time he saw her. "Just remember one thing. You had nothing to do with it. You are not to blame." Sometimes Mr. Compton was really strange.

But when she mentioned this to her mother, right away her mother took his side.

"Bill likes you, Marcy," she said. "He wants to be friends. Try not to judge him too harshly. After all, it's hard for him, too."

This just made Marcy mad. "Hard for him! How come it's hard for him?"

"Things aren't going to be the same for him, either. He's been living alone in an apartment. Now he's going to have to get used to living with you and me."

"But he wants to do that," Marcy pointed out quickly. "He wants to."

"It can be hard all the same. I only ask that you try to be fair."

"But it's not fair! It's not!" Her eyes filled with tears. "He doesn't *have* to do things he doesn't want to. And I *do*!"

Her mother sighed. "At times we all have to do things we don't want to do, honey. I know it's not easy. But things often turn out better than we think they will if only we give them a chance.

"And, Marcy," she added more firmly, "please don't think you're alone. Lots of boys and girls are in the same boat. Bill's children, Roger and Carole Anne, for instance. It isn't easy for them, either—living out in Denver and seldom seeing their father."

Right then Marcy decided she wasn't going to say another word. She didn't want to have to listen to her mother going on and on about the Comptons. She preferred not to think of Comptons at all.

Her mother had told everyone it was going to be just a small wedding, but as it got closer, things certainly seemed to get out of hand. At the last minute even Roger and Carole Anne were coming from Denver.

"Mr. Compton's mother and father are bringing them," Marcy told Wendy.

It was the morning before the wedding, and they were sitting on Wendy's front porch because Kingswood Elementary was over for the year. For Marcy, it was over forever, but she didn't let herself think about this.

"You're going to be related to Roger and Carole Anne," said Wendy.

"I know I'll be related. I'm already related to Ginny's kid."

Her father's new wife had just one child, Joey. Marcy had never met him, but she knew he was little, not even two. Mr. Compton's kids were much older. Roger was fifteen, and Carole Anne was exactly Marcy's age: ten years old.

"By the time Saturday, June 10, is over, I'll be related to five new people," she said.

"How do you figure that?" asked Wendy.

Marcy ticked them off on her fingers. "Mr. Compton, Roger Compton, Carole Anne Compton, and Mr. Compton's mother and dad."

"Mr. Compton's mother and dad! Are you even counting them?"

"Why not? They'll be related."

It occurred to her that her father's wife, Ginny, might have parents. She was about to mention this to Wendy when Aunt Peg stuck her head out the screen door.

"Marcy," said Aunt Peg, "your mother just called. She wants you to go right home."

"What for?"

"All the Comptons are there."

For some reason, as soon as Aunt Peg said this, Marcy got scared. "Can Wendy come, too?" she asked.

But Aunt Peg shook her head. "They don't want to meet Wendy. They want to meet you."

Marcy went down the porch steps and got on her bike and shoved off. Usually she loved riding her bike, especially on a nice day like this with just a little breeze in the air. But today all she could think about was the Comptons.

When she got to the house, she saw Mr. Compton's car parked out front, and she could hear all the laughing and talking as she rode around to the back.

She felt hot and sweaty. Opening the screen door, she went into the kitchen and stood there. There were empty ice trays on the counter and the smell of coffee freshly perked. She wished her mother would come out—or even Mr. Compton. But this was too much to expect. Taking a deep breath, she blew some air up into her face to cool it and walked through the dining room.

When she got to the living room, all the talk stopped, and for a moment she saw only Comptons. Then she felt her mother's arm around her shoulders, squeezing her real tightly. "And *this* is *my Marcy*," she said, as though by just walking into the room Marcy had done something wonderful, as though she had gotten all A's or something like that.

Then Mr. Compton introduced his parents and Roger and Carole Anne. When he came to Carole Anne, he said, "You two girls are going to be great friends."

Marcy kind of nodded and said, "Hi." But Carole Anne didn't say a word.

4

It was a beautiful wedding. All the guests said so, and they were right.

Wendy's mother was matron of honor, and Marcy sat with Wendy and Wendy's father, "Uncle" David, in the first pew on the bride's side of the aisle. Every stitch Marcy had on was brand new: new white underpants with pink ribbons, new slip, new dark blue cotton dress with a big white collar, new white socks and blue shoes. Roger and Carole Anne sat with their grandparents in the first pew on the groom's side, and everything they had on looked new, too.

It was the first wedding Marcy had ever seen, and it was neat. The only part she didn't like was having pictures taken afterward because it took so long. But aside from this, it was fun, especially throwing confetti outside the church and following Mr. Compton's car all decorated with white streamers, with Uncle David blowing his horn.

If only it didn't mean everything was going to get changed, Marcy would have enjoyed it very much.

Maybe this was the way Carole Anne felt about it, too. Every time Marcy looked at her, Carole Anne looked away. The only time she looked at Marcy was when some lady came up to Marcy's mother and said, "Well, how does it feel to be Mrs. Compton?"

Marcy felt Carole Anne looking at her then, and all of a sudden she realized that Carole Anne's mother was Mrs. Compton, too. It also occurred to her that she was still Marcy Benson—the only member of the family with a different last name.

Almost before Marcy knew it, the wedding reception was over and it was time for Mr. Compton and her mother to go off on their honeymoon.

All dressed up in a new suit, her mother didn't even look like herself any more. Marcy felt all hot and sweaty—all dizzy and queer. She hoped Mr. Compton wouldn't kiss her, but he did. Then her mother kissed her and said, "Bye bye, baby. Be a good girl."

Then they got into Mr. Compton's car and drove away.

Riding back to Wendy's house, Marcy and Wendy sat in the back seat of Uncle David's car. Each of them had a slice of wedding cake wrapped in a paper napkin.

"If you put it under your pillow tonight, you'll dream of the man you'll marry," Aunt Peg told them.

"I'm never going to get married," Marcy said.

The next day on the way to the airport, Uncle David told them that the big 747 jet was one of the fastest planes in the sky. It could go up to 35,000 feet and fly at ten miles a minute. It went so high, he said, that Marcy might feel pressure in her ears when the plane came down, and if she did, she should swallow several times.

Marcy found she was swallowing several times on the way up. She could scarcely believe it when the huge plane lifted off the runway and the cars and houses started getting smaller and white wisps of clouds appeared outside her window while her heart continued to pound.

Never had she expected to be taking a plane trip *alone*. Never, in fact, had she expected to be doing any of the things she was doing these days: traveling in jet planes or going out to California or living with her father and Ginny and Joey for four whole weeks! Part of her was happy about all this, but part of her was scared.

At her feet was the black patent leather overnight bag her mother had packed for her.

"It's filled with things to do on the plane," her mother had said.

Marcy had been sure she wouldn't want to do anything but look out the window. However, after about an hour of nothing but white clouds, she hauled the bag up onto her lap and unzipped the zipper.

She was glad she had. Just looking into it made her feel like her old self again.

Her mother had put in a really good selection of stuff: a brand-new spiral notebook, three sharpened pencils, two comic books, a paperback, and, of all things, her dental health book! Why in the world had her mother put that in?

But now that Marcy thought about it, it would be a neat thing to show to her dad. She was really proud of it. She had done it for a science project at school, and just by luck one of her own teeth had fallen out and she had used it to grace the cover, crayoning zigzag lines of pain shooting from it in all directions.

Stapled to the cover was a card bearing the comment, "Outstanding." It had been the only "Outstanding" in Miss MacMannes's entire fourth grade room.

Now she leafed through it, critically studying each page, noting how well each picture was centered, how neat the lettering. Never in her life had she worked so hard on anything, and it was perfect. She couldn't honestly say she would change a thing. It made her wish she were already in California showing it to her father.

But when the flight attendant said, "Ladies and gentlemen, we are approaching San Francisco. The captain has asked that you fasten your seat belts . . ." right away Marcy's heart started pounding in her chest.

How would she ever know which man was her father? Would she really recognize him? That flight attendant was going to think she was some dumb kid, not even knowing who her father was!

But when she got off the plane and went into the terminal, there was her father, ready and waiting for her.

"Hi, Marcy!" he said.

There was no problem at all.

5

The big thing Marcy noticed about San Francisco was that it was all on hills. The houses were squeezed together, and her father and Ginny's house was painted bright red. Instead of doors into the dining room and the kitchen, they had strings of bright colored beads hanging down, and instead of rugs they had straw mats on the floor.

"Who you?" said Joey when she met him.

"Now, Joey," said Ginny, "you know this is Marcy."

Joey just looked at her. Then he said again, "Who you?"

Her father helped her cart her gear upstairs. When he put her stuff down in her bedroom, he turned to her and his blue eyes blazed. "Well, Marcy, what do you say?" he said. "What do you say?"

Marcy didn't know what to say when her father said this, so she didn't say anything.

Then they went down to supper.

Supper was good (delicatessen). With Ginny it was a big thing about the lettuce. She kept saying how it was organically grown. Marcy had never eaten anything organically grown, but the lettuce didn't seem very different. It tasted just the same.

They ate in the kitchen in what Ginny called the breakfast nook. Joey sat in his highchair, and her father and Ginny sat on the bench opposite her, so she had a bench all to herself. She wished Wendy was with her. In fact, what she really wished was that her mother were here. But she didn't let herself think about this.

While they were still sitting at the table, the telephone rang. When her father got up to answer it, the family cat jumped onto the bench and began sniffing around his plate. Ginny didn't try to stop him. She didn't say a word. Her father didn't seem to mind, either. When he came back to the table, he just laughed and said, "Scat!"

Marcy was really surprised. Her mother never would have permitted anything like that.

After supper was over, she said, "My mom said I should help with the dishes."

"We didn't get you out here to work!" said her father.

But Ginny said, "Thank you, Marcy. That will be very nice."

It was interesting helping with someone else's dishes. Ginny had a lot of them already waiting on the drainboard because she didn't believe in loading the dishwasher more than once a day.

"This way I save time," Ginny said. Saving time seemed to be a big thing with Ginny, along with having lettuce and stuff organically grown.

When Marcy finished helping with the dishes, it was getting foggy outside.

"We have fog lots of times in San Francisco," said Ginny.

Marcy stood at the back door looking out at the fog. Now that the dishes were taken care of, she wasn't sure just where she should go or what she should do.

"Would you like to look at TV, Marcy?" asked Ginny.

"Yes," Marcy said.

Her father was sitting on the floor in the living room looking at the TV. He had Joey on his lap. Joey already had on his pajamas and was sucking his thumb.

The picture on TV was about the San Francisco Zoo. Every time a different animal came on, Joey would name it, and her father would make a joke.

"Chimp!" Joey would shout.

"Bimp!" said her father.

"Monkey!"

"Monkey Punkey!"

They didn't see her come in. Then the telephone rang.

Ginny poked her head in from the kitchen. "Marcy, it's for you."

Marcy was really surprised. But then she knew right away it would be her mother.

She went out to the kitchen. Over the wire, her mother's voice sounded far away. "Hi, Marcy. Did you get there safe and sound?"

Just hearing her mother's voice made tears come to Marcy's eyes. "Where are you?"

"Mexico," said her mother. "Mexico City. Did you get there safe and sound?"

"Yes," said Marcy.

"Is the weather nice?"

"Yes."

"I hope you're remembering to help Ginny."

"I am."

"That's a good girl. Today I bought you something nice."

"Did you?"

"Yes. Would you like to know what it is?"

For some reason, Marcy suddenly got mad. "No," she said.

Her mother pretended not to notice.

"You're right," she said. "It's better to keep it a surprise. But it's very, very nice."

Marcy decided not to comment. She didn't say a word.

"Did you find your dental health book?" her mother asked.

"Yes."

"Did you show it to your father and Ginny?"

"Not yet."

"Maybe you can show it to them tonight."

Again Marcy decided not to say a word. It even made her happy to hear her mother get a little mad.

"Well, Marcy," she said, "say hello to Ginny and your father for me. Bill sends his love. Be a good girl."

Marcy didn't answer. As soon as her mother finished talking, she simply hung up.

After she had done this, she could scarcely believe it. She didn't know why she had gotten so mad at her mother or why she hadn't said good-by. She wished the telephone would ring again and it would be her mother on the other end of the line. She wished she knew how to phone her back.

In the living room she could hear Joey giggling. "Lamb!" he shouted.

"Bam!"

She decided she didn't want to show Ginny and her father her dental health book—not right then, at any rate. As soon as the stupid zoo show was over, she said, "May I please be excused? I'd like to retire."

Her father and Ginny looked surprised. She didn't blame them. She must sound like some kind of nut saying she'd like to *retire*. It was the first time in her life she had ever used the word. She hadn't even known she *knew* it.

Not that she cared. She was suddenly good and mad at everybody.

She was already in bed and just about to reach over and turn out the light when there was a tap at her door.

"Hi!" said her father when he came in. He looked all around, as though he hadn't ever seen that room before. "Is everything okay?"

"Uh-huh," said Marcy.

"We're going to leave the light on in the bathroom and your door open a crack in case you want a drink of water or something during the night."

"Okay."

He still kept standing there. "Well," he said, "if there's anything you want, just sing out." He winked. "Anything you don't see, just ask for."

Marcy nodded. She wished he would go.

But instead of leaving, he walked over to the bed and for one awful minute Marcy was afraid he was going to kiss her. But he just clapped his hand down on the top of her head. "Right!" he said, and then turned and walked out of the room.

Seconds later there was another tap at the door, and Ginny came in. "I just wanted to see if you were all settled," she said. She smiled.

"Sure," said Marcy. "I'm fine."

"We're going to leave the light on in the bathroom and your door open a crack in case you want a drink of water or something during the night."

"Okay."

"Well . . ." said Ginny. She, too, looked all around the room, as though she had never been in it. "Well, I guess I'll just say good night."

Marcy nodded. "Good night."

But instead of leaving, Ginny kept standing there.

"Johnnie and I," she said at last, "we're glad you're here."

6

The first thing Marcy saw when she opened her eyes the next morning was Joey standing by her bed.

"Who you?" said Joey.

For a moment Marcy didn't know who he was. Then she remembered and got wide awake. Joey still had his pajamas on, and as she watched, he put the corner of a mangy-looking blanket into his mouth.

"My name is Marcy," she told him. "And you shouldn't put that dirty blanket in your mouth."

To her surprise, Joey instantly took the blanket out. For years Marcy's mother had been telling her to do things or *not* to do things. This was the first opportunity she had ever had to tell somebody else.

She sat up in bed and tucked her hair behind her ears. "Marcy," she said firmly. "Can you say *Mar-see*?"

"Maar-see."

"That's very good, Joey."

Joey had this really goofy kind of smile. He raised his arms. "Up," he said.

Marcy reached down and hauled him up onto her bed. He was heavy, and the bottom of his pajamas was damp. Kneeling on the bed, he put the corner of the blanket into his mouth again.

"Joey . . ." Marcy said warningly.

Instantly he took it out.

Pretty soon Ginny came in. She was wearing her nightgown. As soon as Joey saw her, he scrambled off the bed and ran out of the room.

"I hope Joey didn't wake you up," Ginny said.

"He didn't," said Marcy.

When Joey came back, he was dragging a guitar. "Play me," he told Ginny.

Ginny took the guitar and dropped down on the floor. When she bent her head to tune it, her long hair slid forward and hid her face. Then she raised her head and shook her hair back and started to sing softly about a lady fair who had lost her love. Marcy really liked listening to it. It was neat.

Just as the song ended, her father came in. He was wearing blue jeans that had been cut short. He carried a large box of raisins, some bananas, and a roll of paper towels.

He gave Marcy two paper towels, a banana, and a handful of raisins. Then he sat down beside Ginny on the floor. "Play 'Old Man Mountain,' " he said, and he began peeling a banana for himself and Joey.

It was really fun, sitting up in bed eating raisins and bananas and listening to Ginny play. After she played "Old Man Mountain," she played "Hickory Stick" and something called "Smokey Blue."

Marcy liked watching the way her fingers plucked the strings. "Is it hard to do?"

"Not hard," said Ginny. She smiled. "It just takes time."

Marcy thought about being able to do it. She thought about Wendy watching as she bent over her guitar to tune it, with her hair sliding forward the way Ginny's did. Of course, her hair would have to grow a lot before it could do that.

After Ginny stopped playing, her father said he had to go to work, and Ginny said she had to change Joey. She pulled Joey to her and made a face. "Stinkie, stinkie!" she said.

Joey laughed, and so did Marcy's father.

After they cleared out of her room, Marcy got up and took out her new notebook. Then she climbed back into bed. "Words I Don't Like," she wrote. And underneath: "#1—Stinkie."

She tried to think of some others, but there weren't any she disliked as much as that, so she closed her book and lay back with her hands behind her head.

Her father appeared in the doorway. He now wore long blue jeans and a yellow shirt open at the throat and a brown suede coat. His hair was combed, and his blue eyes blazed.

"So long," he said. "See you tonight."

"Aren't you going to eat breakfast?"

Her father looked surprised. "We just did!"

When Marcy thought about it, she had to admit bananas and raisins made a very good breakfast. And there was the added feature that there weren't any breakfast dishes. All you had to do was put the box of raisins back into the cupboard and throw the banana peels away.

But when she got dressed, made her bed, and went downstairs, she discovered that no one had bothered to put anything away. The box of raisins, the roll of paper towels, and four banana peels sat on the table in the breakfast nook. Above them, two flies were buzzing around.

Marcy looked for a fly swatter but couldn't find one.

In the room above her head, she heard a thump. And then another and another.

Thump. Thump. Thump. She wondered what was happening. She also wondered where the fly swatter was, so she shoved aside the beaded curtains and went upstairs.

The upstairs hall was dark and narrow, but she could see Ginny in the back bedroom. Ginny still wore her nightgown, and the bed wasn't made. Sunlight struck glints in her long shiny hair as her bare feet pumped the treadles and her hands flew busily back and forth at a handloom.

On the floor, in a square of sunlight, Joey lay sound asleep. He had that grimy blanket in his mouth again. Marcy couldn't stand the thought of it. Carefully she eased it out of his mouth.

Ginny laughed. "He won't let me wash it. He likes it that way."

Marcy thought of her mother. It was funny, but when Marcy was home, she almost never thought of her mother. Since she had arrived in San Francisco, however, she seemed to be thinking about her lots of times. One thing for sure, her mother would never let a little kid like Joey tell her what to do. Nor would she leave old banana peels lying around for the flies.

But as she watched Ginny work at the handloom, Marcy forgot about this. Ginny was making a wall hanging. She was weaving all sorts of things into it—birds' feathers, colored sea shells, bright beads. She didn't weave things just for herself, Marcy learned. Her stuff was sold in craft shops all over California. She taught weaving, too, one morning a week at a senior citizens' center.

Once, back at Kingswood Elementary School, Marcy had seen a demonstration of weaving. But she had never known a weaver, and she had never known anyone who could play a guitar. Certainly she had never expected such a person to be related to her.

When the front doorbell rang, Ginny looked up from her work and shook back her hair. "Marcy, will you see who it is, please?"

Marcy went downstairs. When she opened the door, she found a boy standing there.

"Hi," he said. "Johnnie said I should come over today. I'm from next door. You want to come out?"

"I'll have to ask."

When she asked Ginny if she could go outside, right away Ginny said, "Sure, why not?"

She didn't ask where Marcy would be going or what she would be doing or anything like that. She didn't even say, "You better put a sweater on."

Marcy decided she'd better put a sweater on. Then she went downstairs and out the front door.

The boy's name was Tony, and he was one year younger than Marcy—nine years old.

They went through the alleyway between the two houses to a tiny backyard. Tony squatted down in the dirt and drew a circle with a stick. Then he drew a taw line and opened a bag containing marbles.

"I'm not good at this," Marcy told him.

"Johnnie is," said Tony.

It interested her to learn that her father was good at marbles. Knowing this, she tried to play well herself in order to uphold the family name.

That night as they sat in the breakfast nook having supper, Marcy said, "Tony says you're good at marbles, Dad."

She said it, and then she nearly choked. It was the first time she had ever called him "Dad."

Real quickly she looked across the table to see if anyone had taken notice. But her father and Ginny went right on eating, as though nothing peculiar had happened at all.

The only thing different was that under his suntan her father's face got red.

CHAPTER

7

Her father's business was on Powell Street. Painted across the window in big gold letters were the words: BENSON'S, INC.

It interested Marcy to think that, without her ever knowing it, her name had been on a big store in San Francisco all this time.

Under the name, in smaller gold letters, were the words: Stamps—Coins.

Her father was a dealer in rare stamps and coins. He bought and sold them, and some he kept for himself. Her father did all this, but until he took her to work with him one day and unlocked the front door of Benson's, Inc., Marcy hadn't known there was such a business in the world!

"Your grandfather Benson started this business," her father said after he had shown her the big walk-in safe and the locked cases filled with silver coins. "He started me collecting stamps and coins when I was about your age. I thought you might like to start a collection, too."

38

He put a chair behind the counter for her and then presented her with a big white envelope. Down in the lower left-hand corner, printed in red ink, were the words: MINT SET. And, under that, Item No. 937.

When Marcy opened the envelope, she could scarcely believe her eyes. She drew out a shiny black cardboard stamp album and a packet of stamps. There was a whole slew of stamps in the packet, and they were all different colors and kinds: famous persons and owls and ships and trees—all sorts of things.

"These are commemorative stamps," her father told her. "That means they are printed in honor of something." He took a magnifying glass from his pocket. "Study them through this," he said. "My father gave me this magnifying glass when I started collecting. It used to be his when he was a boy. Now it's yours."

Marcy bent over the stamps spread out on the counter before her. She held the magnifying glass above them and looked through the lens just as her father and her grandfather had done. Right then she knew she would keep the magnifying glass forever. It would be her most precious possession.

After that first day, she went down to Powell Street with her father a lot.

She got to know the people who worked for him: Miss Sullivan and Mr. Cotter. She even got to know the regulars who came in, people who wanted Benson's to keep an eye out for particular coins and stamps.

Some of the regulars had been coming to Benson's since Marcy's grandfather's time. Miss Sullivan told her that this was because they knew Benson's was a place they could trust. As the customers came in, her father never once failed to introduce her. "This is my daughter," he would say.

Sometimes one of the regulars would say, "Is she going to come into the business someday?"

And her father would answer, "Maybe so, maybe so."

Marcy had never given much thought to what she would do in life, but now she had this idea in mind that she might be a philatelist, a stamp collector. If she came into the business, that would make three generations of Bensons doing business in San Francisco in the same spot.

She always found plenty of things to do at Benson's, Inc.

Already she had put all her commemoratives into her album, placing them carefully in the correct order. She never got tired of looking at them. With all the colors, they were a beautiful sight.

She could now tick off what they commemorated, too: the poet, Carl Sandburg; Harriet Tubman, the slave who had worked in the Underground Railroad; Captain James Cook, who had sailed his H.M.S. *Resolution* to find a Northwest Passage between the Atlantic and Pacific oceans.

Just going over her collection so much, she had really learned a lot. Owls, for instance. She had four owl stamps. They pictured the great gray owl, the barred owl, the great horned owl, and the saw-whet.

Her American trees offered a giant sequoia, a white pine, a gray birch, and a white oak.

She had four "blocks of fours," as they were called, and thirteen singles for a grand total of twenty-nine stamps in all.

"You can save up your money and buy Mint Sets at the post office for now," said her father. "Later you may want to specialize. You may want to collect only historical personages like Harriet Tubman. Or only topical stamps like your H.M.S. *Resolution*. Or maybe only stamps from a certain country. The important thing is to have a purpose in what you collect. Don't just grab at everything. There's no pride in that."

Soon she had learned enough to do some work for her father.

One day he gave her a large box of United States stamps that he had acquired as part of an estate. They were all stuck together, a mess, and no longer of any value to a collector. It was easy to see that the person who had once owned them hadn't taken pride in them.

Marcy's job was to separate them carefully. On one of the counters, out of the way of customers, she placed the box of stamps, a pan of water, a roll of paper towels, and a pair of tweezers that her father had given her for the job.

First she studied the stamps under her magnifier. It was really surprising the detail the magnifier brought out. Then she soaked the stamps in water. When it seemed as though the adhesive had loosened, she picked the stamps out of the water with the tweezers, gently separated them, and laid them on a paper towel to dry. They could then be used for postage.

Her father paid her the face amount for the stamps: two cents, three cents, five cents, ten cents—whatever the stamp said.

At the end of the day, she counted up her money, put it in an old cash box her father had given her, and stashed it away in the safe.

As the days went by, she kept a record of her money in her spiral notebook. On her best day she had earned $5.52. That was the day she had unstuck 184 three-cent stamps.

8

On Sundays the entire Benson family packed a basket with fruit, bread, and cheese and went somewhere: Chinatown, Fisherman's Wharf, Ghirardelli Square. Once they even took a boat across the bay to the island of Alcatraz, where prisoners used to be kept.

Her father carried Joey strapped to his back. Every now and then, Joey would look at a perfect stranger and say, "Who you?"

Most times people would tell him who they were. Then Joey would say it again.

No matter where they went, Ginny brought her guitar. Marcy knew all of Ginny's songs by heart now: "Hickory Stick" and "Smokey Blue" and lots more.

Marcy no longer sang just any old way. She sang carefully, shaking her hair back, placing the tone.

One Sunday they couldn't go anywhere because Joey's father was coming to visit.

Marcy couldn't have said why, but until she learned that Joey's father would be coming, she hadn't thought about a father for Joey at all.

"Joey's father was Ginny's first husband. Right, Dad?" she said.

"Right," said her father.

"Is he married to somebody else now?"

"No, he's not."

When her father said this, suddenly she had an idea in mind. Even though Tony from next door wanted her to go outside and play marbles, she kept hanging around the house waiting for Joey's father to arrive.

When he came, Joey looked at him and said, "Who you?"

Ginny laughed, but Marcy could see she was nervous. "He says that to everybody, Pete," Ginny said.

Pete didn't laugh. He didn't even smile.

Marcy's father looked at Marcy. "Let's me and you go for a walk," he said.

Walking down the hill, she shoved her hands into the pockets of her blue jeans. "So how come Ginny got a divorce?" she asked.

For the first time since her arrival in San Francisco, she could see her father didn't like what she had said.

He didn't answer for a minute. Then he said, "They just didn't get along."

"Did they get married too young?"

"Maybe."

"Mom said you got married too young to her."

"Did she?"

Inside her pockets, Marcy squeezed her hands tight. She knew she was skating on thin ice, but there was this idea she was trying to get across. She thought that now that everybody was older, Ginny could go back to her husband, her father could go back to her mother, Mr. Compton could go back to his first wife, and everybody would be happy again.

But how could she make all this clear?

"I wish . . ." she said. "I wish you could come back with me when I go."

Her father didn't sound mad any more. "I'll be back, Marcy. I've got to come east this winter. I'll be seeing you then."

"I mean, I wish . . ."

She still couldn't think how to put it, so she decided she'd better not say any more. But right out of the blue, her father said, "That'll never happen, Marcy."

And just the way he said it, she knew it never would. She knew it would never be just her and her mom and him again. In a way she was kind of glad to know it because now she could stop thinking about it.

She was really surprised when, a few days later, her mother telephoned. "It's time for you to come home," her mother said.

"Already?" Marcy exclaimed.

Her mother laughed. "You didn't want to go away, and now you don't want to come home."

Her mother made Marcy mad. The reason she hadn't wanted to go away was because she hadn't known her father then, or what it would be like, or anything about it. It was different now.

In the living room she could hear Ginny playing her guitar the way she did sometimes to calm Joey down before he went to bed. Even without being there, Marcy could see her shining hair falling forward as she strummed a chord. Her father would be sitting in the big wicker chair with a fan-shaped back. Joey would be sitting on his lap, swinging one foot and sucking his thumb.

After she hung up the phone, Marcy shoved through the hanging beads and went into the living room. She put both hands on her hips. She didn't even wait for Ginny to finish her song.

"Guess what," she said. "I have to go home."

9

She was to leave on the 747 jet from San Francisco to Philadelphia on Sunday morning, so on Saturday she went down to Powell Street for the last time. She had to get her cash box out of the safe at Benson's, Inc., and say good-by to Miss Sullivan and Mr. Cotter.

After she told them she would be leaving, there didn't seem to be anything more to say. She got to work unsticking stamps, but somehow things were different. She couldn't think of anything to say to her father on the way home either. It was like the start of her visit, like feeling she didn't know him any more.

Her father didn't seem to care that she was leaving. He hadn't said one word about it. He hadn't said, "I'll call your mom and fix it so you can stay a little longer." He hadn't even been like Ginny, who said her visit had been a total pleasure.

That night after supper she didn't go into

the living room to listen to Ginny play the guitar. She went right upstairs to her room.

Ginny and her father were going out later.

When Joey's baby-sitter arrived, her father tapped at the door of her room. She was still sitting where she had been sitting since she went upstairs—on the edge of her bed.

"We're shoving off now," said her father.

"Okay."

He waited a minute, and then he came over and sat down beside her on her bed.

"What's the matter, Marcy?" he said.

She didn't look at him. "You don't want me to stay."

"Is that what you think?"

She nodded her head. She could feel his blazing eyes.

"Then I haven't done a very good job of making friends with you, I guess."

He got up and walked out of the room.

After he left, Marcy pulled her suitcase out from under the bed and started packing so she'd be ready to go first thing the next morning. Lots of the stuff her mother had packed she hadn't even worn.

After she finished with the suitcase, she opened up her black patent leather overnight case. She planned to keep this right with her on the plane, so into it she put her cash box, her magnifying glass, and her stamp album.

She noticed the comic books and the paper-back her mother had put in for her. She hadn't gotten around to reading them yet. She hadn't had time.

Then she noticed her dental health book. She had never shown it to her father and Ginny. She had forgotten all about it.

She sat down on her bed, picked up her magnifying glass, and studied her tooth. It really looked neat, real big like that. Then she held the glass over the card on which Miss MacMannes had written "Outstanding."

She was about to put the book back into her overnight case when suddenly she stopped. An idea had come to her.

For a while she just sat on the side of the bed and held the book in her hands. Then she set it aside and opened her spiral notebook. She wrote:

Dear Father,
This Dental Health Book is a gift from
your daughter, Marcia Benson.

She studied it a moment. Then she tore that page out and started a fresh one.

Dear Dad,
This Dental Health Book is for you.
Love and xxx,
                    Marcy

She went down the hall to her father and Ginny's room and put the note and the dental health book in the exact center of the pillow on her father's side of the bed.

He couldn't miss it.

10

It was funny that somehow, as soon as she stepped onto the 747, she wanted to get home in the worst way. But once she got there, she really had to wonder what all the rush was about.

The trouble was that her mother had changed. Just in four short weeks her mother had changed entirely. She didn't act like herself any more.

Marcy noticed it the minute she got off the plane—the minute she came up the ramp and saw her mother and Mr. Compton.

Just seeing them standing there together made Marcy mad because they weren't keeping an eye out for her at all. She could have walked right by them, and they would never have known. Her mother was looking up at Mr. Compton, and he was looking down at her, and they were talking and smiling. They didn't even look around until Marcy stopped right beside them and gave her mother a poke.

Then her mother said, real surprised, "Why, it's Marcy!" as though she hadn't expected to see her daughter at all.

But this wasn't the only thing. Everything was changed. Marcy could see this as soon as she walked in the front door of the new house. Even their furniture from the old Morris Avenue house looked different. And not only because it was mixed up with Mr. Compton's furniture. It looked shinier. In fact, if Marcy had one criticism, it was that everything looked too neat and clean.

But this was how Mr. Compton wanted it. Marcy could see that right away.

"Here's the coat closet, Marcy," he said, opening a door in the hallway. "I've had low hooks installed so it will be easy for you to hang up your things when you come in from play or from school. Incidentally, we've agreed it will save the carpet if we all come in and go out by the back door."

Marcy looked at her mother. Her mother certainly had never worried about carpets before. But her mother didn't say a word—not a single word.

At supper that night Marcy was happy to find her absolutely top favorite foods on the new dining room table. After Ginny's organically grown salads, she had forgotten how good her mother's brown bread and home-baked beans could taste.

If she closed her eyes and took a deep breath, the aroma could almost put her right back in the kitchen of good old 9 Morris Avenue. But she didn't get much chance to close her eyes because Mr. Compton kept asking questions about San Francisco all the time. Had she seen the redwood forests? Had she been to Alcatraz? How did she like the cable cars? Stuff like that.

"Incidentally, I've been to Alcatraz," he said.

Mr. Compton was always saying "incidentally," but it certainly surprised Marcy when her mother said it, too. "Incidentally, for dessert we're having Marcy's favorite—chocolate pudding."

Marcy decided right then she was never going to say "incidentally." That was one thing for sure.

In the summertime, back on Morris Avenue, Marcy and her mother usually looked at a couple of TV shows after it got dark. Why not? Marcy didn't have to get up and go to school the next day.

But that night her mother came into the den and stayed for only one show. *One* show. The two of them sat on the sofa together, and it was just like old times. But when the show ended and Marcy said, "So what would you like to see next?" her mother got right up.

"I think that's all the TV I want for tonight," she said. "I think I'll go into the living room and read a book."

"Read a book!" Marcy exclaimed. "What for?"

"*Because*, Marcy, I *enjoy* reading books."

"You never used to before."

"I never had *time* before."

But when her mother went into the living room, she didn't read. She talked to Mr. Compton. Her mother didn't fool Marcy at all.

Later that night after Marcy climbed into bed, her mother came in to kiss her good night—the way she always did. She sat on the side of the bed. "How do you like your room?" she asked.

"It's okay, I guess," said Marcy, and squeezed up her toes real tightly because the room was a lot better than "okay." It had new starched white ruffled curtains at the windows and a new dark blue bandana print quilt on the bed. She really liked it a lot, but for some reason she just plain didn't want to tell her mother so.

Her mother leaned over and kissed her. "I'm glad you're home," she said.

"It's not home!" Marcy burst out.

She really expected her mother to get mad

then. But all she said was, "Well, whatever you decide to call it, I'm glad you're here."

The Dell Lane neighborhood was certainly a lot different from Morris Avenue. Marcy could see this right away when she got on her bike the next morning to have a look around.

Even the names of the streets were different—fancier. Names like Myrtle Way and Crescent Drive instead of Elm Street or Maple. All the houses were new. They were built in different ways, but somehow they all looked the same. They all looked pretty, every single one.

Marcy could see why her mother and Mr. Compton wanted to live here, but personally she liked Morris Avenue. On Morris Avenue the houses were up close to the street, and people sat on their front porches. On Dell Lane there weren't any porches. Things weren't so friendly.

When she got back from her ride, her mother said, "Well, how do you like the place?"

Marcy could tell her mother wanted her to say it was nice, but all she said was, "It's all right."

That night her mother asked her to set the table in the dining room. Marcy was surprised. On Morris Avenue they ate in the dining room only on special occasions. She said, "How come we're eating in the dining room every night?"

"Bill likes to eat in the dining room," her mother replied.

"My father doesn't care where he eats. Lots of times he eats bananas and raisins for breakfast sitting on the floor."

"Does he?" said her mother.

"Yes," said Marcy. "He does. My father doesn't care about which door you come in, either. Or whether you hang up your coat or not."

"Everybody's different."

"Not just different!" She didn't know what had gotten into her. Her breath came in little gasps, and her fists were clenched tightly. "Not just different! Better. My father is better!"

Her mother looked at her. "I'm glad you think so highly of your father, Marcy."

"I don't think highly of my father just because you want me to!"

For a moment there wasn't a sound, and Marcy could hear her words ringing in her ears.

Then her mother said, "Marcy, go to your room."

Marcy's mouth dropped open. It had been

ages, years, since she had been sent to her room.

"Go along. Run upstairs to your room. When you're prepared to be civil, you may come down."

Tears stung Marcy's eyes. She couldn't think of anything terrible enough to say. "I hate you!" she shouted. "I hate this house! I hate him, too!"

"I'm sorry that's the way you feel," said her mother. "Now go to your room."

Going up the stairs, Marcy could scarcely believe it. Everything seemed unreal—being sent upstairs, walking into the unfamiliar bedroom. It was all like a bad dream. She wished she were back in San Francisco with her father. She wished she hadn't come home.

11

A few days later Mr. Compton came back from work looking really happy. He had a letter in his hand. "Good news!" he said. "Good news!" And he smiled right down at Marcy. "You've got a wonderful treat in store for you, young lady. Carole Anne is coming for a visit."

"Oh, Bill, how lovely!" cried her mother. "How nice!"

But Mr. Compton wasn't looking at her mother. "Well now, Marcy," he said. "How do you like that?"

Right away Marcy could see that Mr. Compton thought Carole Anne's visit was the greatest thing in the history of the world. But she honestly didn't know how she felt about it, so she said, "It's okay, I guess."

The next day her mother said, "Marcy, I hope you'll show a little enthusiasm for Carole Anne's visit. Bill and I are counting on you to help us give her a nice time."

"How long is she going to stay?" asked Marcy.

"A month, I believe. Maybe a little more."

"That's a long time."

"Not necessarily. A month goes by quickly if you're having fun. I'm sure your month in San Francisco went very fast."

"San Francisco is a better place than this."

"Well, we don't happen to live in San Francisco, so we can't have Carole Anne visit us there."

"Why does she have to visit us at all?"

Her mother pressed her lips together.

Marcy could see she was skating on thin ice, so she added quickly, "She was just here."

"Just for the wedding. That doesn't count. This is Carole Anne's home too, Marcy. She'll be spending a certain amount of time with us each year, just as you'll be spending time with your father. I hope she'll find it as pleasant to be with you as you did to be with Joey."

"With Joey! He's only a year and a half old!"

"Exactly," said her mother. "Just think how much more companionable you two girls will be."

———

When it was the day for Carole Anne to arrive, they all drove to Philadelphia International Airport to meet the plane.

Marcy couldn't help but notice that it was a lot different from the day she came back from San Francisco.

Waiting in the visitors' section, her mother and Mr. Compton didn't talk to each other at all. They kept their eyes glued to the ramp, and as soon as they saw Carole Anne, her mother said, "There she is! There she is, Bill!" And they both rushed halfway down the ramp and grabbed her from the flight attendant, and Mr. Compton swooped her into his arms.

Not that Marcy had wanted Mr. Compton to swoop her into his arms. It was just that she noticed the reception was sure different for Carole Anne.

After they got back to Dell Lane, Mr. Compton said, "Well now, we'll give you two girls a little time to get acquainted."

And her mother said, "Marcy, why not show Carole Anne your stamp album?"

Marcy led Carole Anne into her bedroom and took her stamp album out of her desk.

Carole Anne looked it over.

Marcy was glad to see that at least she didn't touch the stamps or mess things up.

After Carole Anne got finished looking, she said, "You've got one extra stamp."

Marcy was surprised. She'd been over those stamps a jillion times. "Extra stamp? Which one?"

Carole Anne pointed. "That Christmas stamp. You've got two of them. You should have only one."

Instantly, Marcy could see this was right. Carole Anne was really sharp.

"Can I have it? The extra?" asked Carole Anne.

For some reason, Marcy didn't even stop to think about it. "No," she said right off.

"Why not?" said Carole Anne. "You don't N-E-E-D it. You're S-E-L-F-I-S-H, that's what."

Carole Anne had this habit of spelling things. As the days went by, she would say to Marcy's mother, "Step, may I have some more S-A-L-A-D?" Or, "Step, I just L-O-V-E ice cream."

It got on Marcy's nerves.

Carole Anne also used the word "incidentally." Marcy was the only one at 15 Dell Lane who didn't say that. She didn't call Mr. Compton "Step" either, even though he was her stepfather. She didn't call him anything. She wrote down "incidentally" and "Step" in her notebook after "Stinkie" under "Words I Don't Like."

But what really got Marcy was the way her mother spoiled Carole Anne.

Carole Anne could get away with just about anything—even coming in the front door. And her mother couldn't pretend she didn't know this was happening because Marcy pointed it out to her. "Guess what," she said. "Today Carole Anne came in the front door."

"I suppose she forgot," said her mother.

"No, she didn't. Because I told her she should go around back."

Marcy just stood there waiting to see if her mother would try to wriggle out of that one. And sure enough, smooth as you please, she said, "We have to make allowances for Carole Anne. She has a difficult adjustment to make."

Her mother was getting to sound more like Mr. Compton every day of her life!

"I have a difficult adjustment to make, too," said Marcy.

"I know you do," said her mother sharply. "But I can't say you seem to be making much of an effort. I had hoped that you'd try not to judge people too harshly—that you'd give things a chance. You don't seem to be doing that, and yet Bill and I make allowances for you all the time."

Marcy's mouth dropped open in surprise, and her mother gave a tight little nod. "Yes, Marcy. All the time."

Marcy had to hand it to Carole Anne, though, for being really smart. One Saturday morning they were all in the kitchen unloading stuff from the supermarket, and Carole Anne picked up a bottle of pickles. "Look at this," she said. "Pickles have gone up. Eighty-nine cents is halfway pasted over by a sticker for ninety-nine. That's ten cents."

"And what percent is that, Carole Anne?" asked Mr. Compton.

He was a scientist, so he knew all about percents. Marcy was glad he hadn't asked her.

Carole Anne climbed up on the stool at the kitchen counter and pulled over the memo pad from beside the telephone. Quick as a wink she did some figuring. Then she raised her head. "Eleven percent."

"Right!" said Mr. Compton.

Marcy was interested. She looked up at Mr. Compton. "How do you figure percent?"

Smack in the middle of unloading the groceries, Mr. Compton stopped. "Why, it's the easiest thing in the world!" he cried. "All you have to remember is A over P equals R. Here, sit up on this stool."

Taking the memo pad, he said, "Today the pickles cost ten cents more. That is the *amount* of the increase, so we call that A. The pickles *used* to cost eighty-nine cents, so we call that the *principal*, or P. Now we want to know the *rate* or *percent* of increase, so we call that R. And now we've got A over P equals R."

He marked it out:

$$\frac{A}{P} = R$$

Then he put numbers in place of the letters:

$$\frac{10\cancel{c}}{89\cancel{c}} = 11\%$$

Half an hour later Marcy was still sitting on a kitchen stool beside Mr. Compton and doing percents. She could remember to put A over P, but her answers seldom equaled R.

Every time she got it right, Mr. Compton would say, "Great, Marcy! Great!"

He sounded so pleased she didn't have the heart to tell him that when she got it right it was usually by mistake.

12

With Carole Anne visiting, they had to show her the sights.

Mr. Compton took time off from the lab where he worked, and they went everywhere: down to Philadelphia to see the Betsy Ross house and Independence Hall and the Liberty Bell. Out to Valley Forge to see where Washington's troops had spent the awful winter of '76. To New York City to see the skyscrapers and take a boat ride around Manhattan Island. Even to the New Jersey seashore, so Carole Anne could see the Atlantic Ocean. Because of living in Denver, Colorado, Carole Anne had never seen an ocean in her life.

After she saw it, Marcy said, "So what do you think of it?"

"Oh," said Carole Anne, "I've seen it on TV. I knew what it was like all the time."

One thing Carole Anne *didn't* know was *philately.*

"I've decided to be a philatelist," Marcy told her one day.

She had just received a letter from her father in San Francisco. The letter had some new commemoratives in it, which was what brought the subject up.

"What's a philatelist?" asked Carole Anne.

It pleased Marcy to discover something Carole Anne didn't know. "That's a stamp collector. I'm going to collect stamps, and some day I'm going into the business."

"How can you make any money collecting stamps?"

"After you collect them, you sell them for a higher price. I'm going to be a philatelist out in San Francisco at Benson's, Inc."

She often thought of good old Benson's, Inc. She thought of going down to Powell Street with her father on a foggy morning and looking out the window to watch a cable car go by. She thought of other things, too: eating bananas and raisins, and Ginny playing her guitar, and Joey saying, "Who you?"

She sang the songs Ginny had taught her: "Misery Mountain," "Yes, My Love," "Smokey Blue." She sang softly, placing the tone, shaking back her hair.

Once her mother said, "Why, that's beautiful, Marcy. Just beautiful, dear."

"Ginny taught me," she said curtly.

"Does Ginny have a nice voice?"

"Ginny has a beautiful voice. She plays a guitar. And she can weave, too."

Her mother gave her a kind of funny look. Then she said, "It must be nice to be able to do those things."

Quick as a flash Marcy snapped, "All it takes is time."

She waited then. She knew she hadn't been civil, and she expected her mother to say, "Don't talk fresh." Or maybe even, "Go to your room."

But her mother didn't. She just turned and walked away.

Marcy never knew how it happened, but right from that minute everything seemed to go downhill fast.

One thing for sure, her mother wasn't paying a bit of attention to anyone but Mr. William Compton and Carole Anne. She never corrected Marcy any more at all, even though Marcy knew she was asking for it. She kept talking fresh all the time. It was just as though she couldn't stop herself. And everything seemed to make her mad, like Mr. Compton's saying to Carole Anne every night, "Care to take a walk?"

Every night when he came home from the

lab he said this. And every night her mother said, "Go right along, Carole Anne."

There was hardly one single night that Carole Anne had to help set the table in the dining room. Carole Anne knew she was getting out of it, too. She would look at Marcy as though she could hardly keep from laughing out loud.

But when Marcy brought this to her mother's attention, what did her mother say? She said, "It's important that Carole Anne take these little walks with her father. She'll be going back to Denver soon. This is just his little time to be with her."

"And who is going to help me set the table?"

"For goodness' sake, Marcy!" exclaimed her mother. "I'll help you!"

But the last straw was when Wendy called to ask Marcy if she could come over to Glenview and go swimming in their pool.

Wendy invited *only* her. But when Marcy went to ask her mother if she could go, her mother said, "Yes, but ask if Carole Anne can come, too."

Marcy had never been so mad in her life. "Wendy invited *me*," she said. "Just *me*!"

"That's because she doesn't know Carole

Anne is here. Tell her Carole Anne is visiting. I'm sure she'll want her to come, too.''

''And suppose she says no?''

''Well, Marcy, if she says no, then naturally Carole Anne won't be able to go.''

Marcy raced back to the telephone. ''Wendy,'' she said, ''Carole Anne Compton is visiting here. Do you want her to come too?''

Closing her eyes, she prayed, *Say no, Wendy. Say no. Say no.*

It didn't work.

''Sure,'' said Wendy. ''Why not?''

13

Carole Anne acted as though going to Wendy's was the biggest thing in the history of the world.

"What are you going to W-E-A-R?" she asked.

"Shorts, I guess," Marcy replied.

"I mean what kind of top? What kind of top do you think I should W-E-A-R? Come on into my room and look at my tops."

Carole Anne dumped all her tops onto her bed. Then she dumped out three swimsuits, all bikinis.

"What kind of swimsuit are you going to W-E-A-R?" asked Carole Anne.

Marcy had two tank suits, one black and one dark blue. "I don't know. Wendy doesn't care what people wear."

"Doesn't she?" said Carole Anne.

But the surprising thing was that Wendy did care.

Right away Marcy could see that Wendy

had changed. First of all, she didn't want to be called Wendy any more. She said everybody had to call her "Gwen." And instead of her usual tank suit, she was wearing a new pink-and-white checked bikini. And she had long hair. Marcy couldn't believe Wendy's hair had grown so much in six weeks. Her own hair had scarcely grown at all.

But the worst thing was the way Wendy was showing off in front of Carole Anne. Going through the living room, she pulled a flower out of a vase and stuck it behind her ear. And when she led them upstairs to change into their swimsuits, she said to Carole Anne, "Well, here's my cruddy old room."

Marcy happened to know that Wendy's bedroom had been redecorated only last year in Wendy's favorite colors: yellow and pink. So how come she was calling it a cruddy old room?

After Carole Anne put on her green-and-white striped bikini and Marcy put on her blue tank suit, they went outside. On the way, Carole Anne told Wendy to call her C.A.

"You too, Marcy," said Carole Anne. "Call me C.A."

"I think that's dumb," said Marcy, but Wendy said, "No, it's not, C.A."

When they got out on the patio, that's how Wendy introduced Carole Anne to her mother. "This is C.A."

In the middle of the backyard was a big aboveground swimming pool. They climbed up the ladder and splashed around while Carole Anne kept calling Wendy "Gwen" and Wendy kept calling Carole Anne "C.A."

Then they climbed down the ladder and sat on towels on the grass. Marcy could see she might just as well never have come because all Wendy talked about was Kingswood Elementary and all Carole Anne talked about was her school back in Denver, Colorado.

When Carole Anne mentioned she would be taking French next year, Wendy said, "Awwwk," swallowed twice, and banged her ears.

Wendy always did this when she heard something she couldn't quite believe. "Awwwk!" Swallow, swallow. Bang, bang.

When Wendy said Kingswood Elementary would be offering some ballet in gym class, Carole Anne did the same thing. "Awwwk!" Swallow, swallow. Bang, bang.

Since Marcy was no longer going to Kingswood Elementary and had not yet begun at Wellington, she had nothing to say. But one thing for sure, as soon as she got home, she was going to write "Awwwk!" in her notebook under "Stinkie," "incidentally," and "Step."

It would be a total pleasure.

After a while Aunt Peg got up from where she had been sunning herself on the patio and went in the back door. When she came out, she was carrying a tray of Cokes and cookies, which she passed around.

"Marcy," she said, "your mom tells me you learned some songs out in San Francisco. Will you sing one for us?"

Marcy got all hot and sweaty, and her heart began to pound, but even so, she was glad Aunt Peg had asked her to. Raising her head and shaking back her hair, she sang:

> "Oh, my first love wasn't true,
> Smokey Blue, ah, Smokey Blue,
> Stole my heart and my purse, too,
> Smokey, smokey, smokey Blue."

She sang it softly, hoping she had that far-away look in her eyes that Ginny got when she sang.

When she finished, Aunt Peg said, "Why, Marcy, that was lovely!"

But Carole Anne and Wendy had their hands in front of their mouths and were trying not to laugh.

Aunt Peg frowned. "Gwen, what's the matter with you?"

Making her voice real high and shaky, Wendy sang:

"Oh, my first love wasn't true
Smokey Blue, ah, Smokey Blue . . ."

She didn't know the rest of the words, so she kept singing the same thing over and over, shaking her head the whole time and trying not to laugh.

She looked like some kind of nut. Carole Anne burst out laughing and threw herself down on the grass. So did Wendy when Aunt Peg told her to stop.

Marcy jumped up and ran to the swimming pool. She climbed up the ladder so fast that she jammed a toe on a rung. It hurt, but she didn't care. Wendy was supposed to be her best friend—her very best friend.

As they left Wendy's in the car, Marcy got an idea. Suddenly she wanted to see the old Morris Avenue house in the worst way.

"Can we take a swing by the old house?" she asked her mother.

Through the rear-view mirror, her mother caught her eye. "It's usually better not to go back to a house after you've sold it."

"I want to," Marcy said stubbornly.

"You may be sorry," her mother told her, but she turned the car around.

As soon as they started down Morris Avenue, Marcy knew her mother had been right. She felt this squeezing in her throat. She kept swallowing, as though she were coming down in an airplane, but that didn't help.

When they stopped in front of Number 9, she told herself not to look, but her mother kept saying, "Why, they've painted it blue! . . . Why, they've taken out the hydrangea bed! . . . Why, they've cut down the privet!"

The truth was that 9 Morris Avenue didn't look like itself at all. Neither did Number 11, where Mr. and Mrs. Endicott had lived. The Endicotts' old house was painted brown now. And, of all things, the new people had taken off the front porch! The purple martin house that Marcy had helped Mr. Endicott put up in the backyard was the only thing that had stayed the same.

That night at supper her mother told Mr. Compton about the old house.

"You'd never recognize it!" she said.

She was laughing about it. *Laughing!* She didn't care one bit about their old house at all.

When supper was over, Mr. Compton said,

"I have a suggestion. Let's get the dishes into the dishwasher and then we'll drive over to Meyers' for some soft ice cream."

Marcy helped cart the dishes out to the kitchen, but when it came time to leave for Meyers', she said she didn't want to go.

"What?" said Mr. Compton. "You don't want soft ice cream?"

Carole Anne said, "Awwwk," swallowed twice, and banged her ears.

But her mother didn't say, "Oh, come along with us, Marcy," or anything like that. Her mother didn't say a word—not a single word.

From the window, Marcy watched them leave in the car. They were all smiling.

Then she walked up the stairs to her room. She was glad she hadn't gone with them. The squeezing in her throat was just awful now, and she couldn't keep tears out of her eyes. She kept thinking about the Morris Avenue house and how it used to be when it was just she and her mother together. She kept thinking about Wendy and how she used to be her very best friend.

When she got to her room, she pulled out the chair from her desk, sat down on it, put her head in her arms, and cried.

After she got finished crying, she went into

the bathroom, blew her nose, and splashed water on her face.

Then she went back to her desk, sat down, took out a piece of paper, and wrote:

Dear Dad,
Everything is awful here. Can I come and stay with you?
Love,
Marcy

CHAPTER

14

She folded the letter, placed it in an envelope, sealed it, addressed it to Benson's, Inc., and stamped it with an Einstein commemorative stamp.

Her heart was beating so hard that she thought it would jump out of her chest.

Then she went downstairs, out the back door, and got on her bike. She rode down to the mailbox on the corner of Crescent Drive and Dell Lane and put the letter in the box.

As soon as the box clanged shut, she wished she had the letter back.

Until that minute, she hadn't given one thought to what it might be like living in San Francisco instead of on Dell Lane—what it might be like going to school out there and not being with her mother any more. Now that she thought of it, she couldn't imagine liking such an arrangement at all. Oh, why had she written that letter?

Holding her breath, she carefully tilted the

lip of the box forward. She stood on her toes and stuck her fingers in as far as she could. She felt all around. It was hopeless. The letter was gone.

When her mother and Mr. Compton and Carole Anne came back from getting their soft ice cream, Marcy was sitting in the den.

"Oh, is this where you are," said Mr. Compton.

Outside, she could hear her mother playing the hose on the flower beds. Her mother was laughing at something Carole Anne had said. It was a pretty laugh. Marcy had never noticed it was pretty before.

"If you put a letter in the mailbox, can you get it back again?" she asked.

Mr. Compton opened his newspaper. "As a rule, the United States Postal Service frowns on that. But I guess if you've got a friendly postman, you can get it back. You'd have to hang around the mailbox, though, until pickup time."

"When is pickup time?"

Mr. Compton folded his newspaper in half, the way he always did. "You have to look at the notice on the mailbox," he said. He yawned. "For instance, the next pickup at Crescent Drive and Dell Lane is eleven o'clock tonight."

Marcy's heart sank. She certainly could never hang around the corner of Crescent Drive and Dell Lane until eleven o'clock at night.

She got up and went outside.

"Here's Marcy now!" said her mother.

She smiled at Marcy.

Marcy thought of the letter and felt sick.

Naturally her mother noticed. "What's the matter?" she said.

"I feel sick."

Her mother gave the hose to Carole Anne. She felt Marcy's forehead. Her hand was firm and cool. "You don't seem to have a fever," she said, but she frowned.

When Mr. Compton sauntered out of the house, she said, "Marcy doesn't feel well."

"Maybe too much sun today," said Mr. Compton. "Tell you what, Janet. Why don't you let me finish off the flowers and you tuck Marcia into bed?"

She felt her mother's arm about her shoulders, leading her to the house, hugging her close.

"Hope you'll feel better tomorrow, Marcia," Mr. Compton called after her.

"Me, too, Marcy," Carole Anne sang out. "I hope you'll feel better, too."

Had they all been this nice always? Marcy wondered miserably. How come she was discovering this only now, when the letter was gone? Had she never given them a chance?

The next day was probably one of the greatest Sundays in the history of the world.

The sun was shining, the birds were twittering, squirrels were scampering across the lawn, and downstairs in the kitchen her mother was singing as the delicious aroma of freshly perked coffee wafted up the stairs.

Meanwhile, on a 747 jet flying at ten miles per minute, her letter was getting ever closer to its destination.

Marcy shuddered. Like a prisoner condemned to die in twenty-four hours, she had only this one last day at 15 Dell Lane. By tomorrow, her father would have received her letter and she would be on her way.

"Good morning, Marcia," said Mr. Compton when she appeared at the breakfast table. "How are you feeling today?"

"Fine, thank you," she said.

How pretty the table looked with its blue and white placemats and a bowl of flowers in the center! Until this morning, Marcy hadn't really noticed that the way her mother fixed the table was nice.

After the breakfast dishes were stacked in the dishwasher, they all climbed into the car and headed for St. David's Episcopal Church.

Marcy and Carole Anne sat in the back seat, and Marcy's mother and Mr. Compton sat up front. You could hear church bells ringing in the crystal-clear air.

When Marcy and Carole Anne got out of Sunday School, Mr. Compton said, "I have a suggestion. It's such a nice day, let's take a drive up to New Hope and take a barge ride on the canal."

On the way they played Twenty Questions, and Marcy forgot all about the letter because she had to concentrate. Carole Anne was good at the game. She was really sharp, that girl.

After they took the barge ride, they went to a restaurant with tables set outside. They all had mushroom and sausage pizzas.

Coming home, they sang songs.

"Marcy is the best S-I-N-G-E-R I know," said Carole Anne.

Marcy looked around real quickly. Carole Anne wasn't laughing. She really meant it!

Without even realizing it, Marcy said, "Awwwk," swallowed twice, and banged her ears.

15

The next day Marcy thought about the letter the minute she opened her eyes.

By this time it would be in San Francisco—all ready for the postman who went down Powell Street to Benson's, Inc.

Unless it got lost!

She caught her breath. If only that letter would get lost, she'd do everything her mother wanted her to do for the rest of her life.

When she went down to breakfast, she said, "Do letters ever get lost in the mail?"

"Sometimes," her mother replied.

Marcy crossed her fingers, but she kept an ear out for the ring of the telephone.

She knew, of course, that there was a time lag between Pennsylvania and California. In California her father and Ginny and Joey were still asleep in their beds. It would be three hours before they even got up. She *knew* this. But still she kept listening for the telephone. It was making her sick.

Naturally, her mother noticed. "What's the matter, Marcy?" she said.

Mr. Compton had already gone off to the lab, and Carole Anne was upstairs. It was just Marcy and her mother in the kitchen, and Marcy almost told about the letter then and there. But she changed her mind. Wasn't her mother going to hate her soon enough?

"Nothing," she said.

Her mother looked at her kind of funny. Then she said, "I have a suggestion. Let's go to the mall and buy you a bikini."

"A bikini!" Marcy cried. Her tank suits were practically brand new.

"Well, Carole Anne wears bikinis," said her mother. "And I noticed Wendy was wearing one the other day. I thought you might like one, too."

It was Carole Anne who found her the absolutely perfect bikini in her favorite color: sky blue.

When she put it on and looked in the mirror, she could scarcely believe her eyes. She looked really different. Even her hair seemed to have grown.

"Do you like it?" asked Carole Anne.

"I love it!" Marcy sighed.

After her mother paid for the bikini, she dropped them off at the Y.M.C.A.

The Linden Y was really neat. It had two pools, one indoors and one out. One thing Glenview didn't have for sure was this neat kind of Y.

In her new bikini, Marcy didn't feel like herself at all. It was funny how something like a swimsuit could make you feel different.

"I've decided I don't want to be called Marcy any more," she told Carole Anne as they sat side by side and dangled their feet in the water.

"What do you want to be called?" asked Carole Anne.

Marcy thought a moment. "Well," she said at last. "Step calls me Marcia sometimes."

She looked real quick at Carole Anne. Never before had she called Mr. Compton "Step." But Carole Anne seemed to find nothing strange. After all, Carole Anne had been calling Marcy's mother "Step" for weeks.

"Marcia is a very attractive name," said Carole Anne.

What with the new sky-blue bikini and changing her name, it wasn't hard to keep that letter pushed to the back of her mind. In fact, she had just about decided it had gotten lost when, at suppertime, the telephone rang.

"Marcia, will you answer it, please?" her mother said.

Marcy arose, went into the den, and picked up the receiver.

"Hi, Marcy," said her father. "How are you?"

Just hearing his voice made lightning streaks shoot through her. Her heart started to pound, and her throat went dry. "Fine," she croaked.

"I got your letter. Let me speak to your mother."

Marcy put down the receiver and went back to the dining room. Her legs felt like lead. "Mom," she said. "It's Dad. For you."

Her mother looked really surprised. She got up and hurried into the den.

"Daddy," said Carole Anne, "I'd L-I-K-E some P-O-T-A . . ."

Mr. Compton frowned. "Please be quiet a moment, Carole Anne."

Marcy was glad he told Carole Anne to be quiet because she was straining her ears to listen, too. But her mother was talking so soft and low that she couldn't hear a word.

When her mother came back to the table, her face was white.

"Excuse me," she said. "I don't believe I'll finish supper."

She turned and went up the stairs. Mr.

Compton pushed back his chair and followed her. Marcy was glad he had. She looked across the table. "Oh, Carole Anne!"

Carole Anne's eyes widened. "What's the matter?"

"I think I'm going to throw up."

"Are you sick again?" She jumped up. "I'll get your mom."

"No!" cried Marcy. "Please don't!"

Carole Anne cocked her head to one side. "Well, what then?"

Marcy took a deep breath.

"This is crazy!" exclaimed Carole Anne.

"I've done something awful."

"You have?" said Carole Anne with interest. "What?"

"I wrote my father a letter. I told him I wanted to stay with him."

"So?"

"So that was him on the telephone."

"And?"

"And now I'm going to have to go."

"To San Francisco?"

"Yes."

"And you don't want to?"

Marcy shook her head. "I changed my mind."

For a moment Carole Anne just sat there. Then she said, "I think you should go upstairs and tell your mom."

"Tell what?" asked Marcy anxiously.

"That you changed your mind."

Such an idea hadn't occurred to Marcy. Somehow she had felt that after her father's telephone call and all, she simply would *have* to go to San Francisco. But right away now she could see that Carole Anne had come up with the thing to do.

Going up the stairs, she could hear her heart pounding in her ears. Maybe her mother wouldn't want her to stay now. Maybe she would want her to go away and never come back again.

When she got to the bedroom door, Mr. Compton and her mother looked at her. They were sitting on the side of the bed. Mr. Compton had his arm around her mother's shoulders, and her mother had a piece of Kleenex and was wiping tears from her eyes.

Seeing her mother cry brought tears to Marcy's eyes.

"Oh, Mom!" was all she could say.

She didn't know quite what happened then, but somehow she was in her mother's arms, crying and saying how sorry she was, and that she didn't really want to go away.

Somehow, too, without her even noticing, Mr. Compton had left the room.

Then her mother gave a trembly sigh and said that the very last thing in the world she would ever want would be for Marcy to go away.

"But, Marcy," she added, "you must understand that no one can go back to the way things used to be. It's good to remember the way things were, but it's good to look forward to new things, too—new things to do, new places, new friends." She looked straight at her. "You do see that, don't you?"

Marcy nodded and stood up because she was beginning to feel like some kind of nut sitting there on her mother's lap.

"And you do see," continued her mother, "that if we're going to live happily together, we all must make adjustments. You and I, Bill and Carole Anne—everybody."

"Sure," said Marcy.

She wished her mother would stop talking about it because she really did see, now. In fact, she was good and ashamed of herself.

16

They took Carole Anne back to Philadelphia International Airport on Labor Day. Carole Anne had to get back to Denver because she had to go to school the next day. Marcy would be starting school the next day, also—starting in at Wellington Elementary, a brand-new school.

She tried to look forward to new friends and new things to do, the way her mother had told her, but she got scared every time she thought about these things, so she didn't think about them. Instead, she thought about going out to Denver to visit Carole Anne. She had already been invited. She'd be taking a good old 747 and going out to Denver, Colorado, to visit Carole Anne next summer before she went to stay with her father and Ginny for a while.

When they got back from the airport, Mr. Compton said, "I feel at loose ends."

Marcy knew what he meant. She knew he was missing Carole Anne. She missed her, too. Without Carole Anne around, things wouldn't be the same.

She went to where he sat in his chair. He wasn't reading the paper, or anything. He was just sitting there.

"Care to take a walk?" she said.